my LITTLE PONY
The Cutie Map

Special thanks to Meghan McCarthy,
Eliza Hart, Ed Lane, Beth Artale,
Heather Hopkins, and Michael Kelly.

ISBN: 978-1-68405-065-9
20 19 18 17 1 2 3 4

Licensed By:

www.IDWPUBLISHING.com

MY LITTLE PONY VOL. 9: THE CUTIE MAP. DECEMBER 2017. FIRST PRINTING. IDW Publishing, a division of Idea and Design Works, LLC. Editorial offices: 2765 Truxtun Road, San Diego, CA 92106.
Printed in Canada.

Story by
Meghan McCarthy

Adaptation by
Justin Eisinger

Edits by
Alonzo Simon

Lettering and Design by
Gilberto Lazcano

Production Assistance by
Amauri Osorio

MEET THE PONIES

Twilight Sparkle

TWILIGHT SPARKLE TRIES TO FIND THE ANSWER TO EVERY QUESTION! WHETHER STUDYING A BOOK OR SPENDING TIME WITH PONY FRIENDS, SHE ALWAYS LEARNS SOMETHING NEW!

Spike

SPIKE IS TWILIGHT SPARKLE'S BEST FRIEND AND NUMBER ONE ASSISTANT. HIS FIRE BREATH CAN DELIVER SCROLLS DIRECTLY TO PRINCESS CELESTIA!

Applejack

APPLEJACK IS HONEST, FRIENDLY, AND SWEET TO THE CORE! SHE LOVES TO BE OUTSIDE, AND HER PONY FRIENDS KNOW THEY CAN ALWAYS COUNT ON HER.

FLUTTERSHY IS A KIND AND GENTLE PONY WITH A BIG HEART. SHE LIKES TO TAKE CARE OF OTHERS, ESPECIALLY HER LITTLE ANIMAL FRIENDS.

Rarity

RARITY KNOWS HOW TO ADD SPARKLE TO ANY OUTFIT! SHE LOVES TO GIVE HER PONY FRIENDS ADVICE ON THE LATEST PONY FASHIONS AND HAIRSTYLES.

Pinkie Pie

PINKIE PIE KEEPS HER PONY FRIENDS LAUGHING AND SMILING ALL DAY! CHEERFUL AND PLAYFUL, SHE ALWAYS LOOKS ON THE BRIGHT SIDE.

Rainbow Dash

RAINBOW DASH LOVES TO FLY AS FAST AS SHE CAN! SHE IS ALWAYS READY TO PLAY A GAME, GO ON AN ADVENTURE, OR HELP OUT ONE OF HER PONY FRIENDS.

Princess Celestia

PRINCESS CELESTIA IS A MAGICAL AND BEAUTIFUL PONY WHO RULES THE LAND OF EQUESTRIA. ALL OF THE PONIES IN PONYVILLE LOOK UP TO HER!

The
Cutie
Map

IN PONYVILLE...
...TWILIGHT'S NEW CASTLE IS A NOTABLE ADDITION!
WITH ROOM FOR ALL HER FRIENDS!
IT'S SO NICE, I DON'T KNOW THAT WE SHOULD GO IN...

IT DOES FEEL PRETTY GOOD!
LET'S GO THROUGH THIS ONE MORE TIME.
WE'VE BEEN OVER IT, LIKE, A MILLION TIMES.
WE FOUND ALL SIX KEYS, DEFEATED TIREK, AND GOT THIS SWEET CASTLE.
END OF STORY.

YES, BUT *WHY?*
I DUNNO, *SUGARCUBE*, MAYBE IT'S JUST YOUR NEW HOUSE, AND THERE AIN'T NOTHIN' MORE TO IT THAN THAT.
I MUST SAY, SPEAKING STRICTLY ON AESTHETICS ...IT'S ALL SIMPLY DIVINE.
I AGREE WITH TWILIGHT. AND RARITY AND APPLEJACK AND RAINBOW DASH AND PINKIE PIE.
AND PROBABLY SPIKE.
ZZZZZZZ

AS PRINCESS, I'VE BEEN CHOSEN TO SPREAD THE MAGIC OF FRIENDSHIP ACROSS EQUESTRIA.
SO WHY WOULD THE TREE OF HARMONY WANT US TO SIT IN A CASTLE IN PONYVILLE?
IT DOESN'T MAKE SENSE!
THUT
AS TWILIGHT SITS, HER CUTIE MARK GLOWS...
VVVRRRRRNNNNN
...ACTIVATING THE MARK ON HER THRONE!
CNNNGG

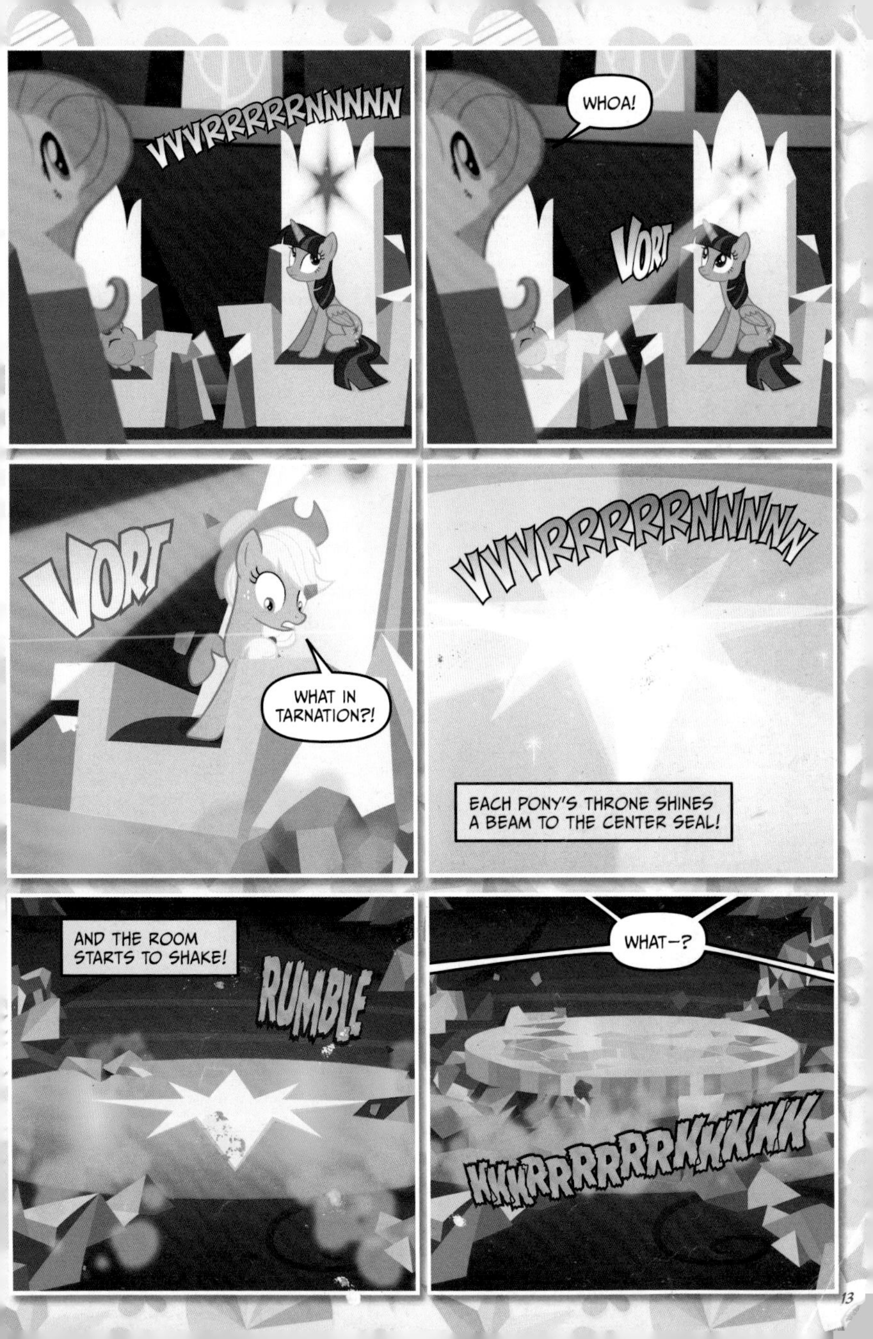
VVVRRRRRNNNNN
WHOA!
VORT
VORT
WHAT IN TARNATION?!
VVVRRRRRNNNNN
EACH PONY'S THRONE SHINES A BEAM TO THE CENTER SEAL!
AND THE ROOM STARTS TO SHAKE!
RUMBLE
WHAT—?
KKKRRRRRRKKKKK

<YAWN!>
DID I MISS ANYTH—
IS THAT NEW?
I LIKE IT.

A SHORT WHILE LATER...
CHOO
"THIS TRAIN WILL ONLY GET US PART OF THE WAY..."
CHOOT CHOOT CHOOOT
WE'RE HERE!
PSSSSSSSSHHHH
AFTER THE PONIES EXIT THE TRAIN, IT DEPARTS IMMEDIATELY!
CHOOOOOOOT
...BUT THERE'S STILL A LONG WAY TO GO NOW THAT WE'RE AT *THE END OF THE LINE.*

ACCORDING TO THIS SCROLL, OUR *DESTINATION* SHOULD BE THIS WAY.
VVRRRNNNN
THIS IS GREAT! WE'RE SO HIGH OFF THE VALLEY FLOOR!
RAINBOW DASH!
SORRY!
WE SHOULD BE RIGHT ON TOP OF IT.
I DO HOPE SO, DEAR.
LOOK, Y'ALL!
IS THAT IT YONDER?
THAT'S IT! THAT'S THE PLACE ON THE MAP!

WELL LET'S GET DOWN THERE AND FIND THE SPA.
WAIT!
VORT
WE DON'T KNOW WHY THE MAP SENT US HERE.
IT COULD BE DANGEROUS.
YES!
STAY BEHIND ME!
I'M ON IT.

SO FAR SO GOOD.
STILL CLEAR.
⟨HRRRK⟩ COME ON! IT'S CLEAR!
SLAMMM

LET'S SEE WHAT WE HAVE HERE...
THIS IS WHERE THE MAP SENT US?!
IT LOOKS LIKE THE *MOST BORING* PLACE IN *EQUESTRIA!*
IT'S JUST AN ORDINARY VILLAGE FULL OF ORDINARY PONY FOLK.
IT COULD CERTAINLY USE A FEW MORE ARCHITECTURAL FLOURISHES...
...OR *ANY* ARCHITECTURAL FLOURISHES.
I THINK IT'S LOVELY.

I DON'T LIKE IT.
I DON'T LIKE IT ONE BIT.
I KNOW SMILES.
AND THOSE SMILES? THEY'RE JUST NOT RIGHT.
FORGET THE SMILES...
...LOOK AT THE CUTIE MARKS!
OKAY, *THAT'S* WEIRD!

AN ENTIRE VILLAGE WITH THE SAME CUTIE MARK?
HOW CAN THAT BE?
I BET THERE'S SOME SORT OF HORRIFIC MONSTER BEHIND IT!
WHAT MAKES YOU SAY THAT?
I DUNNO, 'CAUSE FIGHTING A HORRIFIC MONSTER WOULD BE SUPER AWESOME?
I RECKON WE OUGHTA JUST HEAD INTO TOWN AND TALK TO SOME LOCALS. FIND OUT WHAT'S GOIN' ON.
GREAT IDEA, APPLEJACK, LET'S GO.
THOSE SMILES ARE ***BAAAAD*** NEWS...

AS THE PONIES ENTER THE SMALL TOWN...
WELCOME!
WELCOME!
WELCOME!
THIS MUST BE THE MOST PLEASANT PLACE IN EQUESTRIA!
THANKS A LOT, MAP.

PARDON MY FORWARDNESS, BUT... ARE YOU AN *ALICORN?*
THAT THERE'S THE PRINCESS OF FRIENDSHIP!
WELL YOU'VE CERTAINLY COME TO THE RIGHT PLACE FOR FRIENDSHIP.
WHAT BRINGS YOU TO TOWN?
WE'RE NOT *ENTIRELY* SURE.

I SEE. WELL, ALL ARE WELCOME HERE IN OUR LITTLE VILLAGE.
MY NAME IS DOUBLE DIAMOND AND THIS IS PARTY FAVOR.
HOWDY, DOUBLE DIAMOND.
I'M APPLEJACK, AND THIS HERE'S PINKIE PIE, FLUTTERSHY, RARITY, RAINBOW DASH, AND TWILIGHT SPARKLE.
AND YOU ALL HAVE YOUR OWN UNIQUE CUTIE MARKS.
IF YOU DON'T MIND... HAS THERE BEEN ANY SORT OF TROUBLE HERE LATELY?
TROUBLE?!
WHY, I DON'T THINK WE'VE EVER HAD TROUBLE IN OUR VILLAGE.

PERHAPS YOU'D CARE TO SPEAK TO OUR FOUNDER, STARLIGHT GLIMMER?
I WISH EVERYPONY IN EQUESTRIA WAS AS FRIENDLY AS THESE PONIES ARE.
I'VE GOT MY EYE ON THEM...
SOMETHING'S ROTTEN IN...
...WHATEVER THE NAME OF THIS VILLAGE IS THAT WE'RE IN RIGHT NOW.

A FEW MOMENTS LATER...
STARLIGHT? WE HAVE SOME NEW VISITORS!
KNOCK KNOCK
...THE PONIES CAUTIOUSLY ENTER STARLIGHT GLIMMER'S HOUSE.
WE DON'T KNOW WHAT'S GONNA COME THROUGH THAT DOOR...
BE READY TO FIGHT.
WELCOME!
I'M SO PLEASED TO HAVE YOU HERE.
<SIGH>

THIS IS APPLEJACK, FLUTTERSHY, PINKIE PIE, RARITY, RAINBOW DASH, AND TWILIGHT SPARKLE.
HMMMM...
FORGIVE MY BLUNTNESS,
BUT I'M ASSUMING IT'S *PRINCESS* TWILIGHT SPARKLE?
WE DON'T GET MANY ALICORNS AROUND HERE.
YES. BUT *TWILIGHT* IS FINE.

SO... HOW DID YOU HEAR OF OUR LITTLE VILLAGE?
IT'S KIND OF A LONG STORY. LET'S JUST SAY WE FOUND IT ON A *MAP.*
PINKIE IS QUICK TO ADD HER TWO CENTS!
TECHNICALLY IT'S A TREE-CHEST-CASTLE-MAP.
AND A COLD SCOWL!
WELL, ***HOWEVER*** YOU FOUND US, WE'RE HAPPY TO HAVE YOU.

WE'RE HAPPY TO HAVE ANYPONY WHO WANTS TO EXPERIENCE TRUE FRIENDSHIP FOR THE FIRST TIME.
SAY WHAT?
OH, INDEED. THAT'S WHAT'S SO UNIQUE ABOUT OUR VILLAGE, YOU SEE.
AROUND HERE, WE DON'T FLAUNT OUR SPECIAL TALENTS...
...BECAUSE WE DON'T HAVE ANY SPECIAL TALENTS TO FLAUNT.

IS THAT WHY YOU ALL HAVE THOSE...
...CUTIE MARKS?
PERHAPS IT WOULD BE EASIER TO UNDERSTAND IF I GAVE YOU A TOUR OF THE VILLAGE.
HEADS HIGH, PONIES!
MARCHING PROUD!
WHUMP
LIFE'S A SMILE IN OUR SMALL TOWN.
FOR EVERY FROWN GETS TURNED AROUND!

AND YOU NEVER HAVE TO LOOK AROUND...
...TO SEE THAT WE'RE ALL HERE!
IN OUR TOWN! IN OUR TOWN!
WE DON'T HAVE TO WAIT!
TO FIND OUT THAT OUR DESTINY...
...IS JUST TO EMULATE!
LET'S SEE THOSE BIG, HAPPY SMILES!

IN OUR TOWN! IN OUR TOWN!
WE DARE NOT COMPETE!
WINNING ONLY BRINGS THE WORST, EGO-FILLED CONCEIT.
YOU SEE, NOW EVERYPONY WINS!
LIFE IS A JOY IN OUR TOWN!
WE'RE ALL EQUAL HERE.
NO ONE IS SUPERIOR... AND NO ONE SHAKES IN FEAR.

IN OUR TOWN! IN OUR TOWN!
YOU CAN'T HAVE A NIGHTMARE...
...IF YOU NEVER DREAM.
OTHER PONIES ARGUE... DON'T YOU WONDER WHY?
WHEN YOU THINK THAT YOU ARE SPECIAL, YOU DON'T SEE EYE TO EYE.
IN OUR TOWN! IN OUR TOWN!
EQUALITY IS OUR CUTIE MARK!

YOU'RE KIDDING, RIGHT?
GIVE UP OUR CUTIE MARKS? NO WAY!
RAINBOW DASH, DON'T BE SO RUDE!
I DON'T THINK WE SHOULD JUDGE THEM. THEY ALL SEEM PERFECTLY HAPPY WITH THEIR CHOICE.
DON'T BELIEVE THEIR SMILES, FLUTTERSHY.
I'M SORRY, I GUESS WE'RE JUST A LITTLE CONFUSED BY ALL OF THIS—

WE HAVE NO JUDGMENTS HERE IN OUR VILLAGE.
EACH OF US WAS CONFUSED ONCE, AS WELL...
...BLINDED BY THE FALSE PROMISE OF OUR CUTIE MARKS.
WHOA, WHOA, WHOA–!
IS SHE FOR REAL?
OH.
WHEN WE WERE SENT TO THIS VILLAGE, WE ASSUMED IT WAS TO HELP IN SOME WAY...
...BUT, IT DOESN'T SEEM LIKE YOU *NEED* ANY HELP.

HAVE YOU CONSIDERED PERHAPS THAT YOU MIGHT HAVE BEEN SENT HERE...
...SO WE COULD HELP YOU?
AFTER ALL, NOPONY HAS EVER COME TO OUR VILLAGE AND WANTED TO LEAVE.
WHY SHOULD YOU BE ANY DIFFERENT?

BUT THAT IS ENTIRELY YOUR CHOICE.
PLEASE, ENJOY OUR LITTLE CORNER OF EQUESTRIA.
WE'RE ALL QUITE FOND OF IT.
NO DOUBT YOU WILL BE AS WELL.
DOUBLE DIAMOND, PLEASE HELP OUR GUESTS WITH WHATEVER THEY MIGHT NEED.
OF COURSE!
STARLIGHT GLIMMER TURNS TO WALK AWAY...
WELL THIS WILL CERTAINLY PROVIDE A BOOST TO OUR LITTLE COMMUNITY...
WHEN THE REST OF ***EQUESTRIA*** SEES THAT A PRINCESS GAVE UP HER CUTIE MARK TO JOIN US, THEY'LL FINALLY UNDERSTAND WHAT WE'RE TRYING TO ACCOMPLISH.

A SHORT WHILE LATER...
WELCOME!
WELCOME!
A CUTIE MARK IS A REPRESENTATION OF A PONY'S UNIQUE TALENTS AND SKILLS.
HOW IS IT POSSIBLE TO GIVE THEM UP?
ANY WHY DO THEY KEEP STARING AT US?
IT'S CREEPING ME OUT.
NEED SOMETHING?

NO THANKS—
WE'RE GOOD.
IF WE'RE GOING TO GET TO THE BOTTOM OF WHY THE MAP SENT US HERE...
...WE'LL NEED THE HELP OF THESE PONIES.
I THINK WE RAN OFF TO THE END OF EQUESTRIA BEFORE WE EVEN KNEW WHAT THAT MAP WAS!

IF WE WERE AT THE END OF EQUESTRIA, WE'D BE SITTING ON A BIG A!
GET IT?
REALLY, *MS. PIE*, THIS IS HARDLY THE TIME FOR JOKES.
WE'VE COME ALL THIS WAY AND FOR WHAT?
MAYBE YOU'RE RIGHT, BUT WE'RE HERE NOW.
AND IT SURE *FEELS* LIKE SOMETHING'S WRONG.
IS THIS A BAD TIME?
THAT AND TWO BITS'LL GET YOU A CUP OF CIDER.

WE SHOULDN'T BE BICKERING LIKE THIS IN FRONT OF OUR NEW FRIENDS.
REALLY, APPLEJACK, YOU'RE ALMOST AS BAD AS RAINBOW DASH!
DON'T DRAG ME INTO THIS!
RAINBOW DASH'S SHOUTING CATCHES THE TOWN'S ATTENTION.
IS YOUR FRIENDSHIP ENDING?

ARE YOU CRAZY?
WE'D NEVER LET A DISAGREEMENT GET IN THE WAY OF FOOD!
OKAY, WELL ...UH, MY NAME IS SUGAR BELLE.
WHAT CAN I BRING YOU?
WE HAVE MUFFINS...
...AND... WELL...

THEN I GUESS WE'LL TAKE SIX MUFFINS.
MAKE THAT TWELVE!
WHAT?!
I'M HUNGRY!
SUGAR BELLE STEPS INSIDE TO PLACE THEIR ORDER...
COME ON, GIRLS, WE'VE GOT TO STICK TOGETHER.
IT DOESN'T MATTER WHAT HAPPENED BEFORE; WE'RE HERE NOW.
I GUESS YOU'RE RIGHT.
AND THE SOONER WE FIGURE OUT WHY, THE SOONER WE CAN GO HOME.

WHUP
FORGIVE ME FOR OVERHEARING, BUT JUST A MOMENT AGO YOU WERE DISAGREEING.
AND NOW IT SOUNDS LIKE YOU'RE AGREEING.
UH-HUH.
WELL, YOU HAD SUCH DIFFERING OPINIONS.
AND CUTIE MARKS.
WE HAVE DIFFERING OPINIONS ALL THE TIME, DARLING.

BUT ...YOU LOOK LIKE FRIENDS.
WE ARE FRIENDS.
A SIMPLE DISAGREEMENT WOULDN'T CHANGE THAT...
SUGAR BELLE CATCHES DOUBLE DIAMOND EAVESDROPPING...
I'M SORRY, I'M JUST HAVING A HARD TIME UNDERSTANDING.

DIFFERENT TALENTS LEAD TO DIFFERENT OPINIONS, WHICH LEAD TO BITTERNESS AND MISERY.
CHOMP
SO, WHY AREN'T YOU BITTER AND—
BLECH!
MMM... GOOD...
IT'S ALL RIGHT, I KNOW I'M NOT A VERY GOOD BAKER.
AT LEAST, I'M NOT ANY BETTER THAN *ANYPONY* ELSE IN THE VILLAGE.
AT THAT, *DOUBLE DIAMOND* STANDS UP.

WHICH CATCHES SUGAR BELLE'S ATTENTION.
WELL, I HOPE YOU ENJOY OUR LITTLE VILLAGE!
COME INSIDE BEFORE YOU GO.
MEET ME DOWNSTAIRS.
SUGAR BELLE MAKES SURE SHE WASN'T SEEN...
...THEN DISAPPEARS INSIDE.
ZIP!
OKAY, THAT WAS WEIRD, TOO.

LET'S ALL SIT HERE AND EAT THESE MUFFINS AND ACT NORMAL.
VVVVVRRRRRNNNNN
I *THINK* WE'RE BEING WATCHED.
YA *THINK?!*

NO, NOT LIKE THAT. I MEAN SOMEPONY...
...DOESN'T WANT US TALKING TO SUGAR BELLE.
I GOT AN IDEA.
BUT YOU GOTTA EAT ALL THEM MUFFINS, PINKIE.
WHY ME?!
YOU GOT A STRONGER STOMACH THAN ANY OF US.

AND THAT FILLY IN THERE MIGHT BE OUR BEST CHANCE AT FINDIN' OUT WHAT THE HAY IS GOIN' ON AROUND HERE.
WELL... IF I HAVE TO...
MOMENTS LATER...
CHMMP
I CAN'T BELIEVE YOU ATE ALL OUR MUFFINS, *PINKIE PIE!*

WE BEST GO INSIDE AND GET SOME MORE!
ONCE INSIDE, THE PONIES HEAD DOWNSTAIRS...
NICE WORK, *PINKIE.*
I'VE *ACCIDENTALLY* EATEN CARDBOARD TASTIER THAN THAT.
HELLO? *SUGAR BELLE?*
THANK YOU FOR COMING.

WHY DID YOU WANT US TO COME DOWN HERE?
SO NOPONY COULD SEE WHAT'S ABOUT TO HAPPEN...
WHAT'S ABOUT TO HAPPEN...?
VVVRRRR
TWILIGHT ACTIVATES HER MAGIC...
ARE YOU REALLY THE PRINCESS OF FRIENDSHIP?
DO YOU KNOW PRINCESS CELESTIA? WHAT'S SHE LIKE?

I *LOVE* YOUR CUTIE MARK!
HOW CAN YOU BE FRIENDS WITH DIFFERENT CUTIE MARKS?
DON'T YOU END UP HATING EACH OTHER?
LOOK AT THIS ONE, THIS ONE'S GREAT TOO!
I'D LOVE TO HAVE MY SPECIAL TALENT BACK, EVEN JUST FOR A DAY...
...MAKE SOMETHING BESIDES THOSE DISGUSTING MUFFINS...

SO WHAT'S STOPPING YOU?
GO GET YOUR CUTIE MARKS BACK.
DAYDREAMING IS ONE THING, BUT YOU MEAN... ACTUALLY HAVING IT PUT BACK ON?
THAT SEEMS EXTREME.
I'M NOT SURE STARLIGHT WOULD LIKE THAT.
SHE WANTS US ALL TO BE HAPPY IN OUR SAMENESS.

HOW DO YOU TAKE SOMEPONY'S CUTIE MARK, ANYWAY?
THE CUTIE UNMARKING IS A BEAUTIFUL EXPERIENCE.
STARLIGHT USES THE STAFF OF SAMENESS TO MAGICALLY TAKE THEM AWAY—
—AND REPLACE THEM WITH THESE.

BUT... *NOPONY* SHOULD KEEP YOU FROM YOUR CUTIE MARK.
IT REPRESENTS SUCH AN ESSENTIAL PART OF WHO YOU ARE!
OH, WE'RE NOT KEPT FROM THEM.
THEY'RE IN THE VAULT, UP IN THE CAVES.
WE CAN VISIT ANY TIME WE LIKE TO REMIND US OF THE HEARTACHE OF A LIFE WITH SPECIAL TALENTS.
CAN *WE* VISIT THIS CAVE?

LATER THAT AFTERNOON...
I'M DELIGHTED YOU'RE INTERESTED IN OUR CUTIE MARK VAULT!
WE HOPE SOMEDAY EVERY PONY IN EQUESTRIA WILL MAKE A PILGRIMAGE HERE TO OUR LITTLE VILLAGE...
...TO HAVE THEIRS REMOVED, TOO!
THEN OUR MESSAGE OF PERFECTLY EQUAL FRIENDSHIP CAN FINALLY SPREAD ACROSS THE LAND!
THIS MUST BE THE REASON WE'RE HERE.
PILGRIMAGING?
NO, HELPING THOSE PONIES GET THEIR CUTIE MARKS BACK!
COULDN'T YOU SEE HOW MUCH THEY MISSED THEM?
MAYBE THEY MISSED THEM A LITTLE, BUT EVEN THEY DIDN'T SEEM ALL THAT UNHAPPY.
ARE YOU SURE, TWILIGHT?

THEN WHY DID THEY WANT TO MEET US IN SECRET?
AND WHY DID THEY ASK US NOT TO TELL STARLIGHT WHO TOLD US ABOUT THE VAULT?
"SOMETHING'S NOT RIGHT."
JUST THROUGH HERE!
BEHOLD!

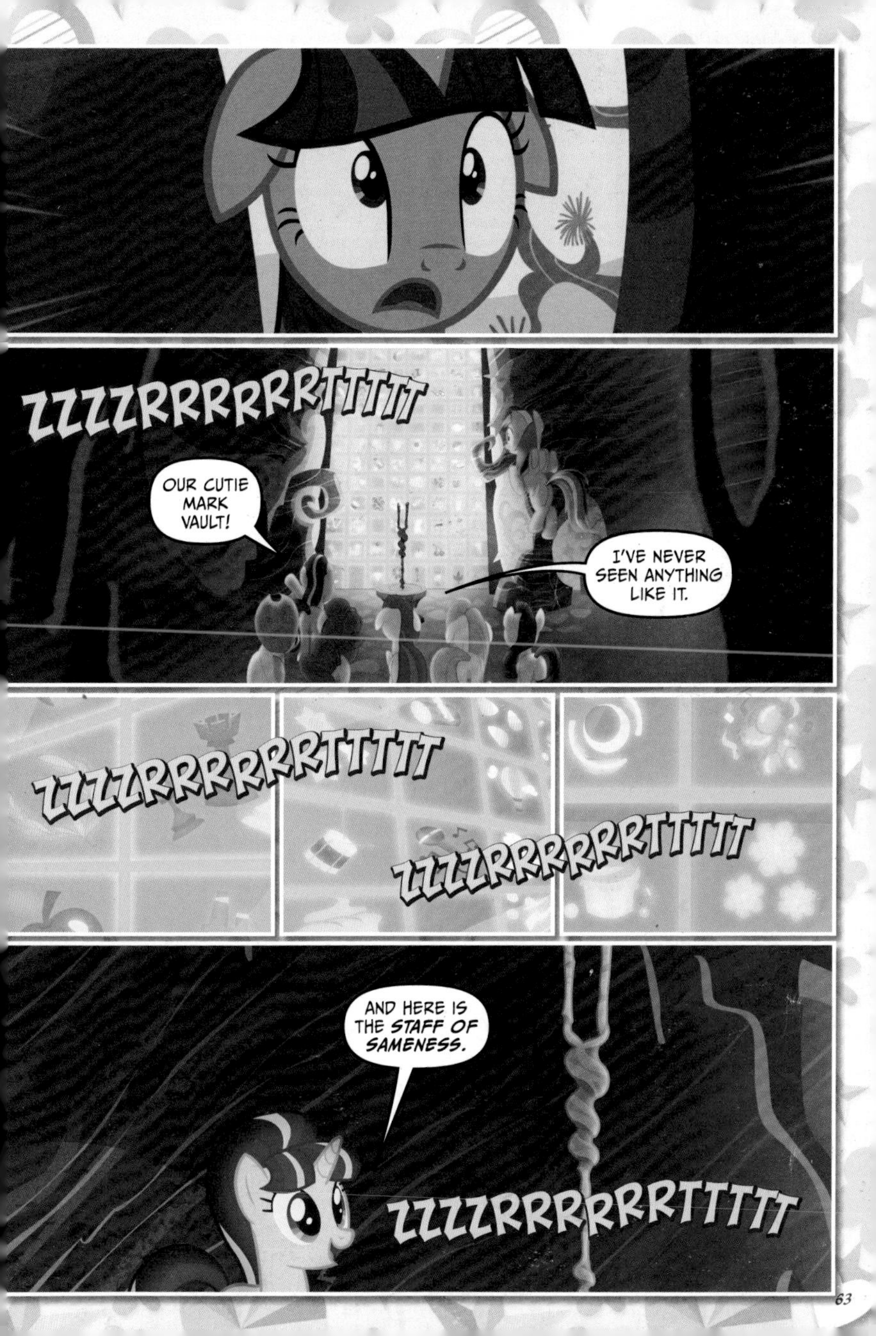
ZZZZRRRRRRTTTTT
OUR CUTIE MARK VAULT!
I'VE NEVER SEEN ANYTHING LIKE IT.
ZZZZRRRRRRTTTTT
ZZZZRRRRRRTTTTT
AND HERE IS THE *STAFF OF SAMENESS.*
ZZZZRRRRRRTTTTT

IT WAS ONE OF THE GREAT MAGE MEADOWBROOK'S NINE ENCHANTED ITEMS.
WE ARE INCREDIBLY FORTUNATE TO HAVE IT HERE.
THIS IS THE TOOL THAT ALLOWS US TO FREE OURSELVES FROM OUR MARKS.
ZZZZRRRRRRRTTTTT
I'M CURIOUS, HOW DID THE SUBJECT OF THE VAULT COME UP?
SOME PONIES WERE TELLING US HOW MUCH THEY MISSED THEIR CUTIE MARKS AND--
HUP

WERE THEY!
WELL IT SEEMS YOU INSPIRE ALL SORTS OF FREE THINKING...
ZZZRRRTTTTT
...DON'T YOU?
WE CERTAINLY DON'T INTEND TO CAUSE ANY DISRUPTIONS TO YOUR CHARMING LITTLE VILLAGE—
GOOD.
LET'S JUST MAKE SURE OF THAT...
...SHALL WE?
THUMP
RARITY TAKES A FEW STEPS BACK...

...AND MORE PONIES COME FROM THE SHADOWS...
HEY!
IT'S A TRAP!
STAY BACK!

VORT
YOU CAN'T—
VIPP
BUT I CAN!
VIPP
UURRRTTTTT
ZORT

THERE, THERE... NO NEED TO STRUGGLE.
ZZZZRRRRTTTTT
THIS WILL ONLY *HURT* FOR A MOMENT.
AAAAGGGGHHHH—
ZRRRRRRP
TWILIGHT'S CUTIE MARK COMES OFF!
IT'S MINE!
ANOTHER FOR THE COLLECTION!

WHAM
ZZZURRRRTTTTT
NOOOOO!
HNNNNNNGG—!
GAH!
ZZZURRRRTTTTT
SOON THEIR CUTIE MARKS ARE ADDED TO THE VAULT TOO!
I DON'T BLAME YOU FOR WHAT YOU DID HERE TODAY.

YOU'VE SPENT YOUR WHOLE LIVES THINKING THOSE MARKS ARE A GOOD THING.
GIVE THEM BACK!
WELL NOW YOU CAN SPEND THE REST OF YOUR LIVES *HERE*...
...WITH US.
AND WE'LL TEACH YOU JUST HOW MUCH BETTER LIFE CAN BE ***WITHOUT*** YOUR CUTIE MARKS.

A SHORT WHILE LATER...
...A LOUDSPEAKER SYSTEM BEGINS TO DELIVER STARLIGHT'S MESSAGE.
IN SAMENESS THERE IS PEACE...
EXCEPTIONALISM IS A LIE...
THE PONIES ARE BEING REEDUCATED!
WHUP WHUP
FREE YOURSELF FROM YOUR CUTIE MARK...
LET US OUT!
HEY, THIS IS PRETTY GOOD.
WE'VE GOT TO FIND A WAY OUT OF HERE.
I CAN'T TAKE MUCH MORE OF THAT VOICE.

OHHH, THIS IS HORRIBLE!
THERE THERE, RARITY, IT'S NOT SO BAD.
YES IT IS!
LOOK AT THESE DRAPES!
I HAVE NO IDEA IF THEY'RE TACKY OR NOT!
WELL I THINK THEY'RE NICE.
SO DO I!
DRIP

OH, THANK GOODNESS!
CAN YOU HELP US, LITTLE BIRDY?
EVEN TWEETS DON'T MAKE SENSE ANYMORE.
WA-BAM
THIS DOOR'S SHUT TIGHTER THAN A... SUMMER OF...
THUD

OF PIGLETS IN...
...SHOOT, I CAN'T EVEN MAKE *COUNTRYISMS* NO MORE!
I DON'T KNOW, MAYBE IT'LL BE SUPER FUN TO BE ALL THE SAME!
SOMETHING ODD ABOUT THAT STAFF.
I HAVEN'T STUDIED EASTERN UNICORNS AS MUCH AS I SHOULD HAVE...
...BUT I'M PRETTY SURE MEADOWBROOK ONLY HAD EIGHT MAGICAL ITEMS, NOT NINE.
AND I DON'T REMEMBER ANY OF THEM BEING A STAFF.
WELL, LOOKS LIKE YOU'LL HAVE PLENTY OF TIME TO THINK ABOUT IT...

INSIDE THE ROOM...
TO EXCEL IS TO FAIL...
...TIME SLIPS BY SLOWLY...
BE YOUR BEST BY NEVER BEING YOUR BEST...
CONFORMITY WILL SET YOU FREE...
ZZZZ
ZZZZ
NNNZZZZ
I'VE GOT IT!
SNORF
I KNOW HOW WE CAN GET OUT!

FORGET IT, TWILIGHT. THIS DOOR'S NOT OPENING.
AND I'M AFRAID THE WINDOWS ARE MUCH TOO SMALL FOR ESCAPE.
BUT THERE IS A THIRD WAY.
OF COURSE! EVENTUALLY THE WIND AND WEATHER WILL WEAR DOWN THE WALLS UNTIL THEY START TO CRUMBLE!
THEN ALL WE HAVE TO DO IS WAIT FOR A BIG ENOUGH HOLE TO FORM AND WE CAN JUST WALK OUT! IT'S THE PERFECT PLAN!
WUM WUM
I GUESS.

WE DON'T ACTUALLY HAVE TO ESCAPE.
THEY'LL JUST LET US OUT WHEN THEY THINK WE'VE ACCEPTED THEIR PHILOSOPHY.
BUT THEY'RE NEVER GONNA BELIEVE WE SWITCHED OVER IN JUST ONE NIGHT.
THERE'S ONE OF US THEY MIGHT BELIEVE...
WELL...?

ME?!
YOU'VE BEEN SAYING HOW GREAT THIS PLACE IS SINCE WE GOT HERE!
THAT'S BECAUSE EVERYPONY'S SO NICE AND THEIR VILLAGE IS SO PRETTY AND... AND...
...OH—
YOU'RE RIGHT. THEY PROBABLY WOULD BELIEVE ME.
I HATE TO LIE TO THEM.
THEY'VE BEEN SO WELCOMING AND FRIENDLY.
ASIDE FROM LOCKING US IN HERE AND TRYING TO BRAINWASH US INTO ABANDONING THE THINGS THAT MAKE US SPECIAL.

OKAY, I'LL DO IT.
BUT WHAT DO I DO ONCE I'M OUT?
YOU'VE GOT TO FIND A WAY TO GET OUR CUTIE MARKS BACK.
EEEK!
KNOCK KNOCK
GOOD MORNING!
I TRUST YOU HAD A PLEASANT NIGHT?
THIS WAY, PLEASE.
THERE ARE SOME *FRIENDS* WHO WOULD LIKE TO SEE YOU.

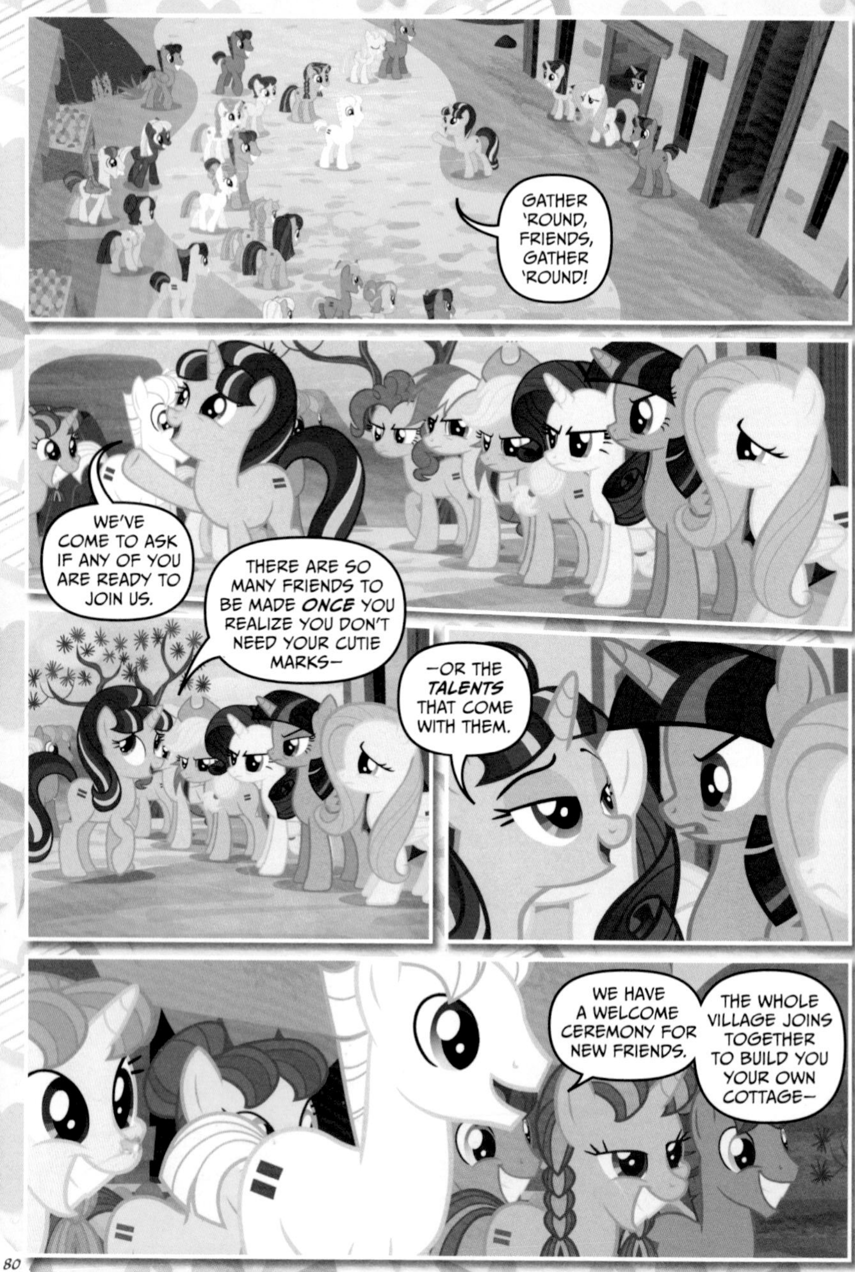
GATHER 'ROUND, FRIENDS, GATHER 'ROUND!
WE'VE COME TO ASK IF ANY OF YOU ARE READY TO JOIN US.
THERE ARE SO MANY FRIENDS TO BE MADE *ONCE* YOU REALIZE YOU DON'T NEED YOUR CUTIE MARKS—
—OR THE *TALENTS* THAT COME WITH THEM.
WE HAVE A WELCOME CEREMONY FOR NEW FRIENDS.
THE WHOLE VILLAGE JOINS TOGETHER TO BUILD YOU YOUR OWN COTTAGE—

NOT INTERESTED.
YOU MAY HAVE THEM NOW, BUT WE'RE *GOING* TO GET OUR CUTIE MARKS BACK!
Y'ALL DON'T UNDERSTAND, DO YA?
YOU CAN'T FORCE NOPONY TO BE FRIENDS! IT DON'T WORK LIKE THAT!
PLEASE, JOIN US!
WE LOVE NEW FRIENDS!
IT'S ALL RIGHT, EVERYPONY, THIS IS A PERFECTLY NORMAL PART OF THE EQUALIZATION PROCESS...

...FOR THOSE WHO HAVEN'T QUITE SEEN THE LIGHT YET.
WE'LL TRY AGAIN TOMORROW.
ONCE YOU'VE HAD A BIT MORE *TIME* TO CONSIDER OUR PHILOSOPHY.
THIS WAY, PLEASE.
HMPH!
PSSST! *FLUTTERSHY!*
ERRR—

I'D LIKE TO JOIN!
WLIP
YEAH!
GREAT!
WELCOME!
FRIENDS!
STARLIGHT GLIMMER GIVES A KNOWING GLANCE TOWARDS TWILIGHT.

HOW COULD YOU?
IF GIVING UP MY CUTIE MARK MEANS I GET TO STAY IN THIS LOVELY VILLAGE...
...WITH THESE LOVELY PONIES, THEN I'LL DO IT.
TWILIGHT TURNS TO GO ALONG WITH THE PLAN...
I DON'T BELIEVE IT!
...WHILE RAINBOW DASH HAMS IT UP FOR THE TOWNSFOLK.

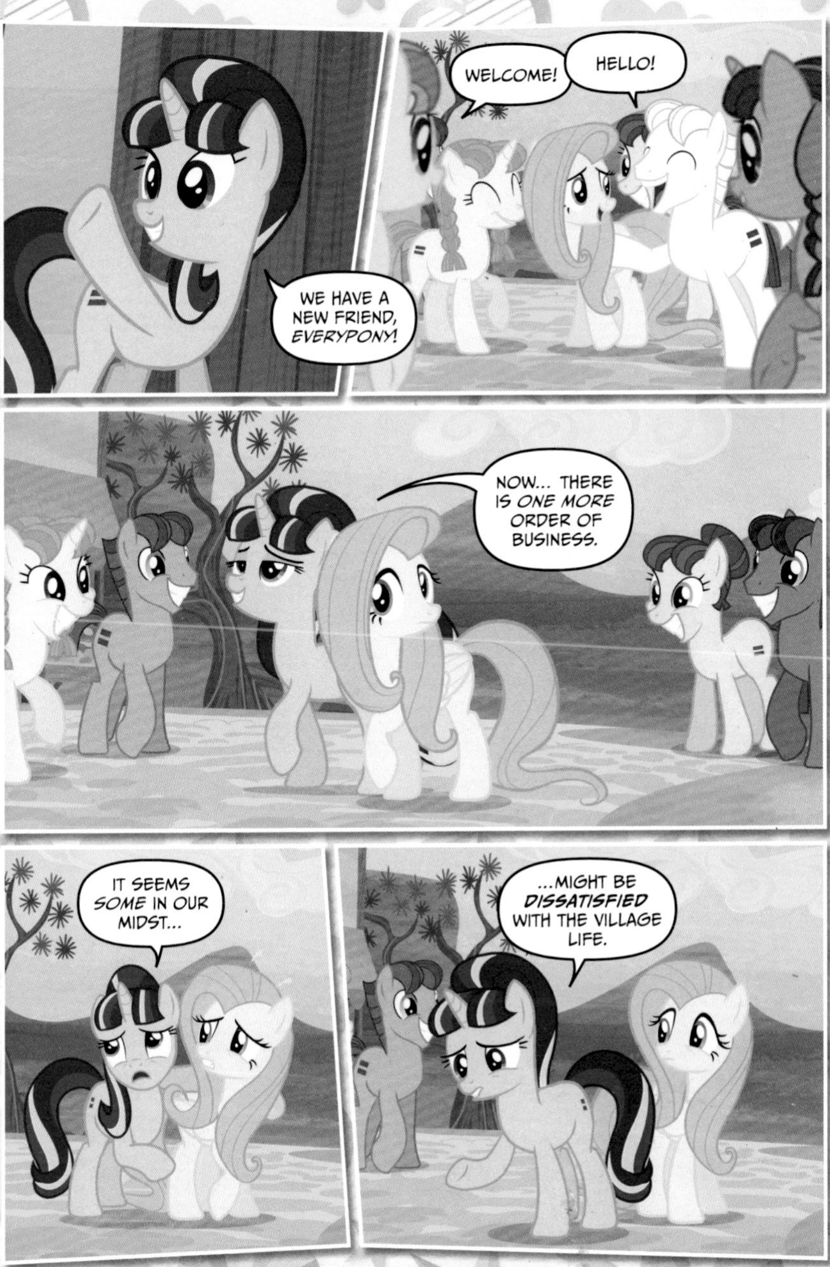

WE HAVE A NEW FRIEND, *EVERYPONY*!
WELCOME!
HELLO!
NOW... THERE IS *ONE MORE* ORDER OF BUSINESS.
IT SEEMS *SOME* IN OUR MIDST...
...MIGHT BE ***DISSATISFIED*** WITH THE VILLAGE LIFE.

GASP!
UNFORTUNATELY IT IS ALL TOO TRUE, MY FRIENDS.
WILL YOU KINDLY TELL US THE NAMES OF THOSE–
–FRIENDS–
–WHO SO DESPERATELY MISS THEIR CUTIE MARKS...
...THAT THEY WOULD SNEAK AROUND IN THE SHADOWS TALKING TO STRANGERS ABOUT IT?

JUST SO WE CAN BE SURE YOUR INTENTIONS ARE, INDEED—
—PURE.
UM... I DON'T KNOW WHO THEY WERE.
I'M SORRY, I DON'T KNOW YOUR NAMES AND FACES YET--

NONSENSE! OBVIOUSLY THESE PONIES MUST HAVE ASKED YOU DIRECTLY...
...KINDLY POINT THEM OUT.
UHHHHHHH—
IT WAS ME!
IT WAS ONLY ME.

I... I ONLY WANTED IT BACK FOR A LITTLE WHILE. I DIDN'T WANT TO KEEP IT.
AND YOU'RE QUITE CERTAIN IT WAS *ONLY* YOU?
I JUST WANTED TO REMEMBER WHAT IT WAS LIKE.
AND NO THOUGHT TO THE PAIN YOU'D CAUSE YOUR FRIENDS.
SUCH SELFISHNESS.
I'M SORRY, *EVERYPONY!*
I NEVER WANTED TO LEAVE THE VILLAGE! I LOVE ALL OF Y—
WHAM

OH NO!
BWAM
WHAT WAS I *THINKING?* I CAN'T BELIEVE I EVEN CONSIDERED ASKING FOR MY CUTIE MARK BACK.
DON'T WORRY, FLUTTERSHY WILL HAVE US OUT OF HERE IN NO TIME.

DIDN'T YOU SEE WHAT JUST HAPPENED OUT THERE?
YOUR FRIEND HAS ACCEPTED OUR WAY.
YOU WILL ALL ACCEPT OUR WAY.
IT'S ONLY A MATTER OF TIME.
HMPF.
FLUMP
THIS GUY'S A BARREL OF LAUGHS.
LAUGHS DON'T COME IN BARRELS.
THEY COME FROM INSIDE YOU AS YOUR BODY'S RESPONSE TO DELIGHT.

SO WHAT ARE WE GONNA DO WHILE FLUTTERSHY'S OUT THERE LOOKIN' FOR OUR CUTIE MARKS?
WE HAVE TO STAY AS POSITIVE AS WE CAN.
IF PARTY FAVOR SEES HOW MUCH WE REALLY DO LIKE EACH OTHER, EVEN THOUGH WE'RE ALL DIFFERENT...
...MAYBE WE CAN USE HIM TO SPREAD OUR MESSAGE TO THE REST OF THE VILLAGE.
TO EXCEL, IS TO FAIL...
LET'S JUST HOPE THEY DON'T CONVERT ANY OF US FIRST.

WELCOME!
HELLO!
WELCOME!
GOSH, YOU REALLY ARE THE NICEST PONIES I'VE EVER MET.
COME, ALL NEW FRIENDS STAY WITH ME UNTIL THEIR COTTAGE IS COMPLETED.
LET'S GET YOU SETTLED...
...AND THEN YOU CAN ENJOY *ALL* THAT OUR *LITTLE VILLAGE* HAS TO OFFER...

LOOKING BACK, FLUTTERSHY SEES THE CONCERNED PONIES...
...AND STARLIGHT NOTICES!
HMM.
–!
EVERYTHING ALL RIGHT?
OH VERY MUCH!
THEN JUST COME RIGHT ON IN AND WE'LL MAKE YOU AT HOME.

THAT NIGHT...
POOF
KAFF
KAFF
GET THE CUTIE MARKS BACK.
THAT'S ALL YOU'VE GOT TO DO, FLUTTERSHY.
JUST SNEAK THROUGH THE DARK...
...UP TO THAT SPOOKY OLD CAVE WITH THE SCARY MAGICAL STAFF...
GET THE CUTIE MARKS BACK.

MOMENTS LATER...
OKAY, YOU'RE DOING GREAT.
THE CAVE'S GOT TO BE CLOSE NOW...
EXCELLENT WORK, DOUBLE DIAMOND.
OF COURSE. BUT I DON'T UNDERSTAND...
WHY YOU WANTED ME TO BRING THEM HERE?
FLUTTERSHY IS ONE OF US NOW, SURELY SHE CAN BE TRUSTED.

THIS ONE BELONGS TO A PRINCESS.
IT COULD BE VERY IMPORTANT TO OUR CAUSE.
BUT IF TWILIGHT SPARKLE BECOMES OUR FRIEND...
...THEN WHAT DO WE CARE ABOUT THIS OLD CUTIE MARK?
I JUST WANT TO KEEP THEM CLOSE. UNTIL EVERYTHING IS... SETTLED.
?!
YOU MAY GO, DOUBLE DIAMOND.

<GASP!>
FLUTTERSHY DISAPPEARS AROUND THE CORNER AS DOUBLE DIAMOND EXITS...
FWIP
...BUT HER CURIOSITY GETS THE BEST OF HER!
OH DEAR!
HOW AM I EVER GOING TO GET THE CUTIE MARKS BACK NOW?

OW!
FLUSTTERSHY FOLLOWS THE NOISE UPSTAIRS...
CLUMSY FOOL!
SPLISH
ALWAYS CLEANING UP MY OWN MISTAKES.
ZZZRRRTTTTT
WHAT?!
NO?!

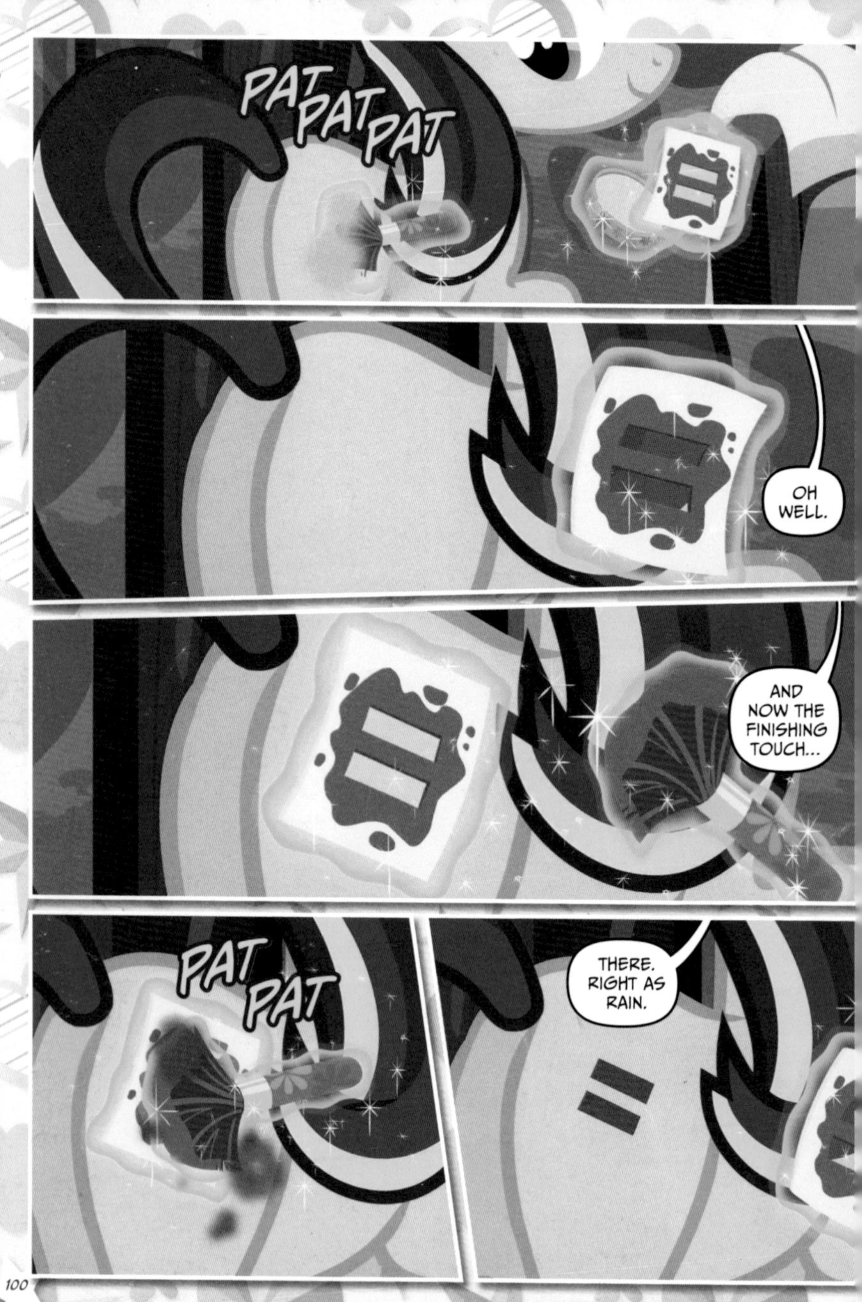
PAT PAT PAT
OH WELL.
AND NOW THE FINISHING TOUCH...
PAT PAT
THERE. RIGHT AS RAIN.

<GASP!!>
STARLIGHT FREEZES! DID SHE HEAR SOMETHING?
NOPE!
I COULD HAVE SWORN I HEARD SOMETHING.
OH NO!

THE NEXT MORNING.
I'VE GOT A GOOD FEELING ABOUT TODAY!
SO... DO ANY OF YOU HAVE ANYTHING YOU'D LIKE TO SAY?
A PITY. WELL, LET'S TRY THIS AGAIN TOMORROW, SHALL WE?

NO NEW FRIENDS TODAY, I'M AFRAID!
WAIT!
I'D LIKE TO LOCK THEM IN.
MARVELOUS, FLUTTERSHY, THAT'S THE SPIRIT!
PARTY FAVOR, WILL YOU JOIN US PLEASE?
GRONK
I'M SORRY, STARLIGHT!
I'M SORRY, EVERYPONY!

I'VE SEEN THE ERROR OF MY WAYS!
I NEVER WANT TO LOOK AT MY CUTIE MARK AGAIN!
IT SEEMS THERE IS CAUSE FOR CELEBRATION AFTER ALL!
THEY TRIED TO BREAK ME!
THEY WOULDN'T STOP TALKING ABOUT HOW DIFFERENT THEY ARE—
—AND HOW THAT SOMEHOW MAKES THEIR FRIENDSHIP STRONGER!
BUT I DIDN'T LISTEN!
SUCH BACKWARDS THINKING!

I KNEW WHAT THEY WERE UP TO AND I DIDN'T LISTEN!
WELL DONE, PARTY FAVOR!
WE *WELCOME* YOU BACK WITH *OPEN* HOOVES.
UM, STARLIGHT?
I THINK WE MIGHT HAVE ONE MORE FRIEND JOINING US TODAY.
OH MY!
WOW!
CAN IT BE?

IS THIS TRUE?
I... I THINK SO.
BUT I JUST WANT TO BE SURE.
IF I AGREE TO LEAVE MY CUTIE MARK IN THE VAULT, I'LL REALLY BE HAPPIER?
JUST LOOK AROUND! EQUALITY HAS GIVEN *US* MORE HAPPINESS THAN *YOU'VE* EVER KNOWN!
AND YOU WOULDN'T LET ME JUST LIVE HERE IN THE VILLAGE WITH MY OLD CUTIE MARK?

OUT OF THE QUESTION.
A PONY WITH A DIFFERENT CUTIE MARK IN OUR MIDST WOULD DESTROY OUR ENTIRE PHILOSOPHY.
WE ARE ALL EQUAL HERE!
OH YEAH?!
THEN HOW DO YOU EXPLAIN THIS??
WOOSH
SPLISH

WHY WOULD YOU DO THAT? THAT WASN'T VERY NICE!
I KNEW YOU COULDN'T BE TRUSTED.
BUT IT'S TOO LATE!
DRIP
SCRUB SCRUB
NO!
GET AWAY!

DON'T BE AFRAID!
EVERYTHING WILL BE OKAY—
—EEEE!
WHAT ARE YOU LOOKING AT?
THEY'RE THE PROBLEM, NOT ME!

I GUESS WE'RE NOT ALL EQUAL IN YOUR TOWN.
HOW COULD YOU?
YOU SAID CUTIE MARKS WERE EVIL.
YOU SAID SPECIAL TALENTS LEAD TO PAIN AND HEARTACHE.
THEY DO, DON'T YOU SEE?
LOOK AT THEM!

WHY DID YOU TAKE *OURS* AND NOT GIVE UP *YOUR OWN*?
I HAD TO, YOU FOOLS!
HOW COULD I COLLECT YOUR CUTIE MARKS WITHOUT *MY* MAGIC?
BUT... THE STAFF... THE STAFF HAS ALL THE MAGIC WE NEED--
THE STAFF IS A PIECE OF WOOD I FOUND IN THE DESERT!
IT'S MY MAGIC THAT MAKES ALL THIS POSSIBLE!
YOU'D ALL STILL BE LIVING YOUR MISERABLE LIVES, THINKING YOU'RE BETTER THAN *EVERYPONY* ELSE, IF IT WEREN'T FOR MY MAGICAL ABILITIES!

I BROUGHT YOU FRIENDSHIP!
I BROUGHT YOU EQUALITY!
I CREATED HARMONY!
YOU LIED TO US!
SO WHAT? EVERYTHING ELSE I SAID IS TRUE!
THE ONLY WAY TO BE HAPPY IS IF WE'RE ALL EQUAL!
EXCEPT FOR *YOU*!

WHAT DID YOU SAY?!
ZZZZRRRTTTTT
EVERYPONY HAS UNIQUE TALENTS AND GIFTS.
AND WHEN WE SHARE THEM WITH EACH OTHER, THAT'S HOW REAL—

QUIET!
YOU CAN'T HAVE THAT CUTIE MARK, STARLIGHT.
EITHER WE'RE ALL EQUAL OR NONE OF US ARE.
SHE'S RIGHT.
?!
IT'S NOT FAIR.

UH...
...UMMM...
STARLIGHT REALIZES MAYBE SHE'S *NOT* IN CONTROL...
ZZZRRRTTTTT
ZORT

STOP HER!
SHE'S GETTING AWAY!
CLOP CLOP CLOP
COME ON, LET'S GO GET OUR CUTIE MARKS BACK!
RUMBLE
YEAH!
IT'S ABOUT TIME!

COME ON! LET'S GET OUR CUTIE MARKS BACK!
OUR CUTIE MARKS AREN'T IN THE VAULT.
THEY'RE IN *THERE*... WITH HER!
MEANWHILE, AT THE VAULT.
THUD
IT WON'T OPEN!
THUD
STAND BACK, EVERYPONY!

CLOP CLOP CLOP CLOP
FA-
-WHIP!
KKRRAKK
THE CRACK SPREADS ACROSS THE VAULT!
KKRRAKK

BAW
OOSH
AND THE CUTIE MARKS ARE FREE!
ZIP
ZAP
ZORT
VORT
VVVVRRRRRRNNNNNNNN
THE VILLAGERS ARE TURNING BACK TO NORMAL

ZIP
ZORT
VVVVRRRRRRRNNNNNNN
I FEEL GREAT!
I HAVEN'T FELT THIS WAY IN AGES!
CLOP
CLOP
CLOP
CLOP
CLOP
CLOP
WOW!
EVEN WITHOUT MY CUTIE MARK, I CAN TELL THIS IS BEAUTIFUL.

MEANWHILE, ALONE INSIDE HER HOME...
...THEY THINK THEY CAN COME TO MY VILLAGE AND DISRUPT MY LIFE?!
LET'S SEE HOW THEY LIKE SPENDING THE REST OF THEIR LIVES WITHOUT THEIR PRECIOUS CUTIE MARKS!
ZZZRRRTTTT
STARLIGHT LIFTS THE BED AND REVEALS A HIDDEN PASSAGE!
CLOP CLOP CLOP

TROUBLE GETTING INSIDE?!
WE CAN HELP!
STAND BACK, EVERYPONY!
FWOOOOOSH
CLOP
CLOP
CLOP
BWHAMM

CHECK EVERYWHERE!
THEY'RE GONE!
THEY WERE RIGHT OVER THERE!
LOOKS LIKE SHE WENT THAT WAY.
WELL WE'VE GOT TO GO AFTER HER!

AND THEY DO!
EMERGING FROM A CAVE JUST OUTSIDE TOWN.
LOOK!
STARLIGHT GLIMMER FOLLOWS A NARROW MOUNTAIN PASS TOWARDS ESCAPE.
CLOP CLOP CLOP
I HAVE AN IDEA...
HEY!

PSSSSSHHHHHHHHH
PARTY FAVOR GETS TO WORK!
FWIP
FWIP
FWIP
I SEE HER!
SHE'S HEADED FOR THE PASS.
IF SHE MAKES IT INTO THOSE MOUNTAINS...
WE'LL NEVER FIND HER.
THOSE ARE *AMAZING*!

THERE'S A WHOLE NETWORK OF CAVES UP THERE.
YOUR CUTIE MARKS WILL BE GONE FOREVER.
THEN LET'S GET MOVING!
THE PONY'S NEW FRIENDS RACE TO THEIR AID!
FLAP FLAPFLAP FLAP
CLOP CLOP CLOP
BUT THE FRIENDS FROM PONYVILLE AREN'T AS FAST AS NORMAL...
AW, COME ON! I CAN BARELY FLY THIS SLOW!
UP AHEAD...
CLOP CLOP CLOP
NIGHTGLIDER APPROACHES...
FWOOOOSH

ARE YOU ALL SO WILLING TO GIVE UP EVERYTHING BECAUSE OF THESE... STRANGERS?!
ZORT
BOOOSH
AHH—!
A PILE OF SNOW GROUNDS *NIGHTGLIDER.*
DOOOOF

WE GAVE UP EVERYTHING FOR YOU! BECAUSE WE THOUGHT YOU WERE OUR FRIEND!
CLOP
CLOP
FARTHER BEHIND...
I CAN'T BELIEVE WE HAVE TO COUNT ON THESE OTHER PONIES TO SAVE OUR CUTIE MARKS!
IF WE HADN'T COME HERE TO HELP THEM, THEY'D STILL BE LIVING UNDER HER RULES!
NOW IT'S THEIR TURN TO HELP US!
AND I KNOW THEY CAN DO IT!

CLOP CLOPCLOP
THEY CAN'T CATCH ME.
OH NO!
SUGAR BELLE GETS AN IDEA FROM HER CUTIE MARK!
OH YEAH!
FWHIP
TIME FOR MY NEWEST RECIPE...

SNOW PIE!
UNGH!
KRRRRRRK
BUT THE CUTIE MARKS FALL OFF THE CLIFF!
THUD
NO!
ZZZRRRTTTTT

STARLIGHT GLIMMER CATCHES THEM JUST IN TIME!
ZZZZZRRRRRRTTTT
YOU CAN'T STOP ME!
VORT
SHE BLEW UP THE BRIDGE!
KA-BLAMMM
WHAT'LL WE DO?!
CLOP CLOP CLOP CLOP

FWIP FWIP FWIP FWIP
BUT IT CAN'T STOP PARTY FAVOR...
BOING
THERE YOU GO!
...AND HIS BALLOON BRIDGE!
COME ON!
BOING
BOING
SHE'S GOING TO GET AWAY!

SKREEEEEEEE
WAIT A SECOND...
THESE ARE MY OLD SKIS.
THIS IS WHERE I FIRST MET STARLIGHT.
MAYBE YOU CAN REMINISCE ANOTHER TIME.
SHE'S ALMOST TO THE CAVES!
FEEL LIKE AN *AIR-DROP?*

I'M ALMOST THERE!
NOT IF I CAN HELP IT!
SWOOOOOOSH
SWOOOOOSH
A BIG WAVE OF SNOW BREAKS FREE UNDERNEATH DOUBLE DIAMOND...
CLOP CLOP CLOP
NO!

SHE MUST BE UNDER THAT SNOW!
ZZZRRRRTTTT
STARLIGHT'S MAGIC FADES AND THE JARS FALL TO THE GROUND...
KRSHHHHH
KRSHHHHHH
KRSHHHHH
...FREEING THE CUTIE MARKS!
IS THAT...?!
VOOOOOOSH
VVVVRRRRRNNNNNN

VOOOOOOSH
VVVVRRRRRNNNNNN
YEE-HAW!
FINALLY, I CAN BUCK LIKE A FIVE-BIT SNAKE HERDER IN AN APPLEOOSA RANCH HOUSE AGAIN!
AND YOU GOT YOUR *COUNTRYISMS* BACK, TOO!
LOOK!
AHH—!

I'LL SHOW ALL OF YOU!
VVVVVRRRRRRTTTTT
TWILIGHT ARRIVES JUST IN TIME!
STAY BEHIND ME!
VVVRRRRRNNNNN
VIPPPPPPPP

SHE CAN'T HURT US?
VIPPPPPPPP
STARLIGHT HOLDS HER FIRE...
IT'S OVER, STARLIGHT.
I STUDIED THAT SPELL FOR YEARS! HOW CAN YOU—?
I STUDIED MAGIC FOR YEARS, TOO, BUT WHAT I DIDN'T KNOW THEN—
—WAS THAT STUDYING COULD ONLY TAKE ME SO FAR.

EACH OF MY FRIENDS HAS TAUGHT ME SOMETHING DIFFERENT ABOUT MYSELF.
IT WAS THEIR UNIQUE GIFTS AND PASSIONS AND PERSONALITIES THAT HELPED BRING OUT THE MAGIC INSIDE OF ME.
I NEVER WOULD HAVE LEARNED THAT I REPRESENT THE ELEMENT OF MAGIC WITHOUT THESE FIVE.
AND I CERTAINLY WOULDN'T BE HERE TO STOP YOU NOW.
SPARE ME YOUR *SENTIMENTAL NONSENSE.*
I GAVE THESE PONIES REAL FRIENDSHIPS THEY NEVER COULD HAVE HAD OTHERWISE!
HOW DO YOU KNOW THAT?
YOU NEVER EVEN GAVE US A CHANCE.

ZZZRRRTTTTT
ZZZRRRTTTTT
FLASH
SHE'S GETTING AWAY!
WE'LL NEVER FIND HER IN THERE!

WE JUST HAVE TO HOPE THAT WHEN SHE'S HAD A CHANCE TO THINK IT OVER...
...SHE REALIZES THAT YOU ALL HAVE TAUGHT HER SOMETHING.
IT'S *YOU* WHO HAVE TAUGHT US SOMETHING.
WE ALL CAME TO THIS VILLAGE BECAUSE WE WERE SEARCHING FOR SOMETHING MISSING FROM OUR LIVES.
WE THOUGHT STARLIGHT HAD GIVEN IT TO US, BUT NOW...
...NOW IT SEEMS IT WAS IN FRONT OF US ALL ALONG.

IT'S US!
WE WERE MISSING FROM EACH OTHER'S LIVES.
SQUEEZE
DOES THAT MEAN YOU'LL STAY IN THE VILLAGE?
IT'S OUR HOME. I'M NOT GOING ANYWHERE.
AND I FINALLY HAVE A CHANCE TO BAKE SOMETHING BESIDES TERRIBLE MUFFINS!
THIS IS A CHANCE FOR ALL OF US TO GET TO KNOW EACH OTHER AGAIN FOR THE VERY FIRST TIME.
TEE-HEE
HA HA
GIGGLE

A SHORT WHILE LATER...
THE VILLAGE RETURNS TO NORMAL.
CATCH!
ENJOY!
NOW THOSE ARE REAL SMILES.
WUH-OH!
VRRRRN-VRRRRNNN

I'LL NEVER GET USED TO THAT.
I THINK IT'S DIVINE.
DOES THAT MEAN THE MAP IS CALLING US SOMEWHERE ELSE?
I HAVE A FEELING IT MEANS OUR WORK HERE IS DONE.
LOOKS LIKE YOU WERE RIGHT, TWILIGHT. THE MAP DID HAVE A REASON FOR SENDIN' US HERE.
WE BROUGHT REAL FRIENDSHIP TO THESE HERE PONIES.
BUT THE MAP DIDN'T SEND ME.
IT SENT *US.*
THERE'S NO DOUBT YOU'RE A PART OF MY MISSION TO SPREAD FRIENDSHIP, TOO.
AWWWWWW!!
SQUUEEEEEEEEZE
NOT THE END !